Wild Animals!

By Eduardo Bustos

Illustrated by
Lucho Rodríguez

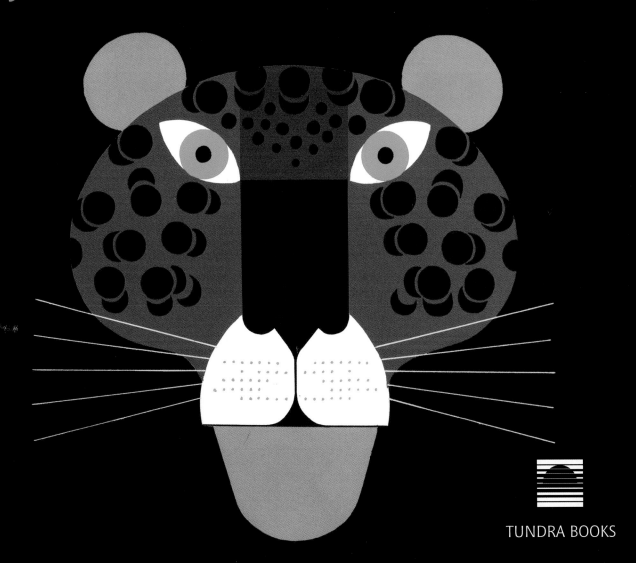

TUNDRA BOOKS

Hippopotamus:

I wallow in the mud to cool
myself under the African sun.
I may look sleepy, but watch
Only the rhinoceros and the
whale are larger than me. I a

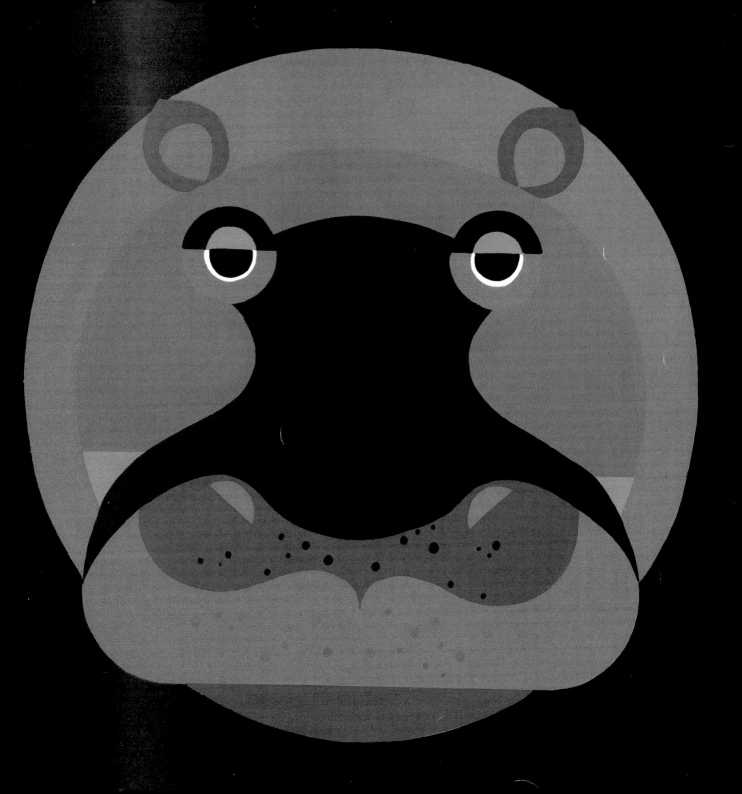

Yak:

I live high up in the mountains of Central Asia where it gets very cold. My fine, heavy coat and its special undercoat keep me bundled up and warm, even when the storms come.

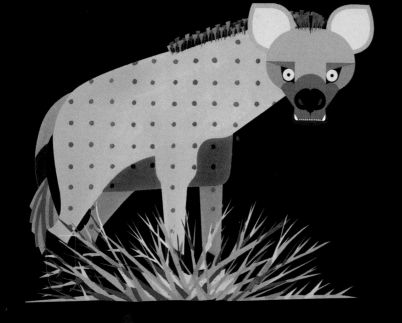

Hyena:

Whether I roam the plains or the cool mountains of Africa, you can hear my strange and haunting cry. Do I sound like I am laughing? Perhaps, for I am a fine and speedy hunter.

Koala:

My home is in Australia. My fur is soft and my ways are gentle. I carry my babies on my back as we feast on the leaves of the eucalyptus tree. Just like hands, my fingers grip the branches to keep me safe.

Leopard:

I am the smallest of the Big Cats: the lion, the tiger, and the jaguar. I live in Africa and Asia – I don't mind places that are hot or cold. Though my legs are short, I am a swift runner.

Sloth:

I am a creature of South America's rain forest. I eat buds and shoots, insects and small mammals, but, still, I must conserve my energy. I move slowly, slowly, and I spend so much time hanging upside down that my fur grows in the opposite direction than it does for most animals.

Fox:

Do you think I look like a dog? We are related, but I am not happy in a pack. I am a solitary creature — wherever I live around the world.

Spectacled Bear:

I am the only bear that lives in South America. In my treetop home, I can munch all day on leaves and insects. Do I look like I'm wearing glasses?

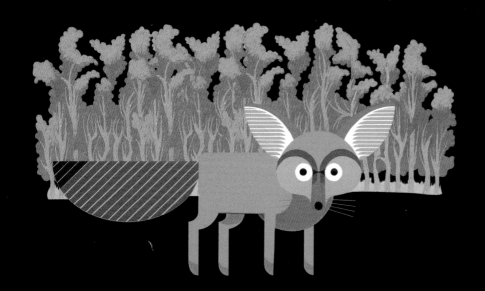

Fennec Fox:

My fur-covered paws protect me from the fiery Sahara sands, and my sandy-colored coat helps me blend in. I come out at night to catch the insects that I can hear with my incredibly huge ears.

Spotted Owl:

My enormous eyes rest during the day, but at night, I'm perched up in a tree, scanning the ground beneath me. You'll find me in North America, but don't try to creep up behind me because I will see you. My head can turn almost all the way around.

Lion:

Once I roamed the whole world, but
now my home is only in parts of Africa
and Asia. I like the grassland, where
I and other lions hunt together for
the game we eat. Although I love the
savanna and grassland, I sometimes
take to the bush and forest.

¡Qué animales! copyright © 2007 by Ediciones Tecolote, Mexico
First published in this edition by Tundra Books, Toronto, 2009

English translation copyright © 2009 by Tundra Books
Cover and interior illustrations reproduced with permission of Ediciones Tecolote

Published in Canada by Tundra Books,
75 Sherbourne Street, Toronto, Ontario M5A 2P9

Published in the United States by Tundra Books of Northern New York,
P.O. Box 1030, Plattsburgh, New York 12901

Library of Congress Control Number: 2008910200

Library and Archives Canada Cataloguing in Publication

Bustos, Eduardo
    Wild animals! / written by Eduardo Bustos ; illustrated by Lucho Rodríguez.
Translation of: ¡Que animales!
Interest age level: For ages 2-5.
ISBN 978-0-88776-946-7
    1. Exotic animals–Juvenile literature.
2. Animals–Juvenile literature. I. Rodríguez, Lucho
II. Title.
QL49.B8813 2009   j590   C2008-907201-4

We acknowledge the financial support of the Government of Canada through the Book Publishing Industry Development Program and that of the Government of Ontario through the Ontario Media Development Corporation's Ontario Book Initiative. We further acknowledge the support of the Canada Council for the Arts and the Ontario Arts Council for our publishing program.

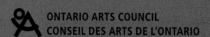
ONTARIO ARTS COUNCIL
CONSEIL DES ARTS DE L'ONTARIO

Design by Leah Springate

Printed and bound in Singapore

1 2 3 4 5 6   14 13 12 11 10 09